D1414656

For Christen, my light, thank you for you.
For Tali and Gabe who share their joy and smiles each day!
And to Marty Sleeper and the Runkle School community—
many thanks for your kindness and support!

And to Steve Fraser—many thanks!

First Aladdin Paperbacks edition August 1999

Text copyright © 1999 by Eric Arnold
Illustrations copyright © 1999 by Sean Taggart

Aladdin Paperbacks
An imprint of Simon & Schuster Children's Publishing Division
1230 Avenue of the Americas
New York, NY 10020

Designed by Steve Scott
The text for this book is set in Caecilia.
The illustrations were rendered in pen and ink.
Printed and bound in the United States of America
2 4 6 8 10 9 7 5 3

Library of Congress Cataloging-in-Publication Data
Arnold, Eric H., 1951–
Jokes you shouldn't tell your teacher / by Eric Arnold.
p.   cm.
Summary: A collection of riddles and jokes relating to school,
in such categories as "Getting Ready for School,"
"Overheard in the Hallway," and "Recess."
ISBN 0-689-82698-2 (pbk.)
1. Riddles, Juvenile. 2. Wit and humor, Juvenile. [1. Schools—
Wit and humor. 2. Riddles. 3. Jokes.]   I. Title.
PN6371.5.A75   1999   818'.5402—dc21
99-18088   CIP

Getting Ready for School!

Dad: Did you take a bath this morning?
Jack: No, why? Is one missing?

Alligators get their teeth cleaned by opening wide and letting the plover bird pick the meat between their teeth.

Mom: We don't have any more pancakes for breakfast!
Charlotte: How waffle!

In China, way back in 1498, the first bristle toothbrush (much like the ones we use today) was used. The bristles were plucked from the backs of hogs! Sounds refreshing, doesn't it?

If you're looking for a rich, creamy milk for your cereal, head to Lapland. Reindeer milk is the richest milk of any domesticated animal. But, grab your scuba gear if you want to taste the richest milk of all—the milk of the killer whale! It's nearly nine times richer than cow's milk.

Little sister: Eeee-yikes!
What's that fly doing in my cereal?
Big brother: The backstroke!

All insect bodies are divided into three parts: the head, the thorax, and the abdomen. Insects also have six legs (three pairs!).

Ray: What kind of orange can float?
Melissa: A naval orange.

Is a spider an insect? It does look like one, but it isn't. It has eight legs and it also has two body parts instead of three.

Big brother: What do you want
with your cereal?
Little sister: Milk!

Going to School!

Daniel: What are students called
who ride the bus?
Kaneeta: Passengers.

Wilson: How do students get to school
in the fall?
Abby: Autumn-obile!

The tallest tree in the world is the sequoia. It can grow more than three hundred feet tall. One of the shortest trees, and you better get your binoculars out, or maybe a microscope, is the snow willow. It is only one inch tall.

Nate: Why did the girl ride her horse to school?
Julia: Because her horse was too heavy
to carry!

Principal: Did the bus arrive on time?
Johnny: No, it arrived on the road.

Principal: Tommy, are you late for school again?
Tommy: No, I'm early for tomorrow!

Principal: Why was the bus so late this morning?
Bus Driver: It was hugging the road!

Overheard in the Hallway!

Kelly: Why are you crying?
Ashley: Jacob said my writing was tear-ible!

Paul: Why did the elephant
come back to school?
Rachel: He wanted to get an education
so he could get a better job. He was tired of
working for peanuts.

Steve: How did the elephant get
into the school?
Kevin: It opened the door.

Ruth: What's that elephant doing in
the hallway?
Sarah: About three miles an hour!

When school is out, an elephant might take a visit to Florida, but not to go to Disney World. It would go see its close relative, the manatee. The loveable manatee lives underwater and is a vegetarian. It averages about ten feet in length and weighs up to one thousand pounds.

Pedro: Did you hear about the duck that was flying upside down?
Katherine: No.
Pedro: It quacked up!

LaMont: What's a teacher's favorite candy?
Crystal: Chalk-olate!

Rich: What's wrong with your pencil?
Jonah: It got a lead-ache!

Principal: How can we keep the students from charging in the hallway?
Assistant Principal: Take away their credit cards!

Ben: You sure talk a lot. I wish you could be more like a shoe.

Carlos: What do you mean by that?

Ben: Well, a shoe has a tongue, but it doesn't say a word!

Ben: Did you hear about the pet rabbit in Ms. Haddad's science class?

Carlos: Yeah, it got sick.

Ben: So what did Ms. Haddad do?

Carlos: She took it to the hopital!

Stan: Where can I find my notebook?

David: It depends on where you lost it!

The great white shark's teeth never stop growing. Its front teeth wear down and fall out. But new teeth, which had formed in the back of the jaw, now move up to take the place of the missing teeth.

Geography!

A Geography Test

1. What part of London is in France?
   —*n*

2. Where do fish like to go on vacation?
   —Finland

3. What is the best city to go bike riding in?
   —Wheeling (West Virginia)

   What are the five longest rivers in the world?
   (answer below)

4. In what state capital can you find the most rabbits?
   —All-bunny (New York)

Nile (Africa); Amazon (South America); Mississippi-Missouri (United States); Yangtze (China); and the Ob-Irtysh (Russia).

9

5. What is the best state for buying a new soccer shirt?
   —New Jersey

6. Where were the first french fries made?
   —in Greece

7. What country's restaurants do the best business?
　　　　　　　—Hungary

Can you name the seven continents?
(answer below)

8. In what country does a person never walk?
　　　　　　　—Iran

9. What is the best mountain to climb to get a good night's sleep?
　　　　　　　—Mount Ever-rest!

Mount Kea in Hawaii is actually taller than Mount Everest! It's an underwater mountain, and if you measure it from the bottom of the ocean floor, it's 32,000 feet—3,000 feet taller than Everest!)

10. What city is the best place to get sick in?
　　　　　　　—Baltimore, M.D.

Africa, Antarctica, Asia, Australia, Europe, North America, and South America. Asia is the largest and Australia is the smallest.

11

11. What state is round on both sides but high in the middle?

—Ohio

What country has the "Great Wall?"
(answer "A" below)

12. What people enjoy the end of a geography test the most?

—the Finnish (In Finland)

13. Where is the last place you want to go for a relaxing vacation?

—Mount Rushmore

Can you name the presidents whose faces are carved on Mount Rushmore?
(answer "B" below)

14. Which tourist site should you stay away from in Paris?

—I-fell Tower!

A: China.   B: George Washington, Thomas Jefferson, Abraham Lincoln, and Theodore Roosevelt.

Check out these world-famous landmarks on a map—the Eiffel Tower, Gateway Arch in St. Louis, Washington Monument, and the Statue of Liberty. Can you rank these in order from the tallest to the shortest?

(answer below)

15. What is the best country to buy a baseball cap?

—Hat-i

16. What is the best state to get school supplies?

—Pencil-vania

What's the page number of this page? Thirteen, right? Well, if being on page 13 makes you a little nervous, you might have triskaidekaphobia (TRIS-KAH-DECKA-FOBIA) —fear of the number 13!

17. Where does Zorro buy his clothes?

—Cape Cod, Massachusetts

Eiffel Tower (984 feet), Gateway Arch (630 feet), Washington Monument (555 feet), and last, but not least, the Statue of Liberty at 305 feet!

18. Where is the safest place to keep money in America?

   —The Outer Banks in North Carolina

19. What people are the fastest runners in the world?

   —the Russians

20. Where is it impossible to be locked out of your house?

   —the Florida Keys

*Three pairs of states border each other
but do not have any letters in common.
What are these three states?*

(answer below)

Jacob: I have an uncle who lives in Alaska.
Maria: Nome?
Jacob: Sure, I know him, he's my uncle!

Alabama/Tennessee; Ohio/Kentucky; Utah/Wyoming.

In what city can you go to two different restaurants on two different continents?

(answer "A" below)

Katie: I have an aunt who lives near one of the Great Lakes.
Matthew: Erie?
Katie: Not really, but she is a little strange!

What is the name of the only state whose name shares no letters with its capital?

(answer "B" below)

Steph: You need to draw the equator on your map.
Jodi: I will when I get around to it!

Billy: In what city can you get the best desserts?
Molly: San Francisco—because it has the Golden Gate Fridge!

A: Istanbul, Turkey, which straddles the continents of Europe and Asia.
B: Pierre, South Dakota.

If you think fortune cookies were invented in China, that's an unlucky guess! They were invented in San Francisco in the early 1900s by a gardener at the Japanese Tea Gardens in Golden Gate Park.

Billy: What do people in Australia call little black and white cats?
Molly: Kittens.

The seven highest mountain peaks (known as the "Seven Summits") on each of the seven continents are:

1) Asia: Everest at 29,028 feet

2) South America: Aconcagua at 22,834 feet

3) North America: McKinley (also known as Denali) at 20,329 feet

4) Africa: Kilimanjaro at 19,340 feet

5) Europe: Elbrus at 18,510 feet

6) Antarctica: Vinson Massif at 16,067 feet

7) Australia: Kosciusko at 7,316 feet

Steph: Where is the shortest bridge in the world?
Jodi: On your nose!

The three longest suspension bridges in the world are:

1) Akashi Kaikyo Bridge in Japan
   (12, 831 feet long)

2) Humber Bridge in Humber, England
   (4,626 feet long)

3) Verrazano Bridge in New York City
   (4,260 feet long)

From the Library!

Avi: Reading always makes me hungry!
Patrick: What kinds of things are you reading?
Avi: Menus.

*Where is the largest comic book collection
in the world?*

(answer "A" below)

Samuel: Why is the library the tallest room in
the school?
Mr. Hathaway: It has the most stories.

What is the tallest building in the world?

(answer "B" below)

A: In the Library of Congress, Washington, D.C.
B: It's the Petronas Twin Towers in the city of Kuala Lumpur,
the capital of Malaysia. The twin towers were completed in 1996
and are thirty-three feet taller than the Sears Tower in Chicago.

Kathy: How did the librarian catch the students reading books?
Sean: With bookworms.

Randy: I had a dentist appointment this morning. Sorry I missed your book report.
Billy: Oh, it was nothing.
Randy: That's what I heard!

Kathy: Why are you taking the librarian's pulse?
Sean: I want to make sure she has good circulation!

In the movie The Wizard of Oz, *what was Dorothy's last name?*
(answer "A" below)

Mr. Hathaway: What are you doing with that pile of books on cars?
Samuel: My teacher told me to pick out an auto-biography!

What was Alice's last name in Alice in Wonderland?
(answer "B" below)

A: Gale. Why do you think the author of the Oz books, Frank Baum, chose the last name "Gale" for Dorothy?
B: She didn't have a last name.

Kathy: I just read the best fantasy book!
Sean: What was it about?
Kathy: It was about this fairy princess who could get anything she wanded!

What was Mark Twain's real name?
(answer below)

Kathy: Why is the last row in the school auditorium so cold?
Sean: Because it's Z-Row!

Mr. Hathaway: Why are you laughing so loud? You're reading a very sad and serious book!
Andre: But, Mr. Hathaway, there's a comma-dy on every page!

Samuel Langhorne Clemens. He took his pen name from a Mississippi River boat term that meant "two fathoms deep."

Computers!

Tommy: How do you catch a runaway computer?
Rachel: With an Internet!

Sonya: What's the difference between a computer and a piece of paper?
Aleks: You can't make a spitball out of a computer.

Wanda: What kind of portable computer does a rabbit like to use?
Jevon: A lop top!

Tommy: Why do you keep a piggy bank in front of your monitor?
James: It's my screen saver!

Wanda: What should I do after my computer starts running?
Jevon: Chase it!

~~Spelling!~~ Spelling!

Gabe: What ten-letter word starts with g-a-s?
Juanita: a-u-t-o-m-o-b-i-l-e.

What's the fastest land animal?
(answer below)

Kristin: What can spell every word in every language?
Manny: An echo!

Tali: What two letters can keep you from doing your homework?
Gabriel: TV!

Mr. Tomashiro: Sandy, why did you write a ten-foot-long letter *S*?
Sandy: You said we had to write a long letter in class!

The cheetah—it can run more than seventy miles per hour!

Mr. Tomashiro: What do a volcano and the moon have in common?
Randy: The letters o and n (and craters!)

What's the largest land animal?
(answer "A" below)

Mr. Tomashiro: Is there any word in the English language that contains all the vowels?
Rakeem: Unquestionably!

Mr. Tomashiro: Why are you pasting letters of the alphabet all over the hamster cage?
Jevon: Because it's our class's *alpha-pet.*

Mr. Tomashiro: What letter is at the end of everything?
Jevon: *g*

Where does Thursday come before Wednesday?
(answer "B" below)

A: The African elephant grows nearly twelve feet tall and weighs up to seven tons!   B: In the dictionary.

David: Which is larger—a watermelon or a grapefruit?
Ricky: They're the same! They both have ten letters!

Mr. Tomashiro: How do you spell "Massachusetts"?

Eduardo: M-a-s-a-c-h-u-s-e-t-s

Mr. Tomashiro: I'm sorry, that's not how you spell it.

Eduardo: But Mr. T., you asked me how I spelled it!

What is the largest animal in the world?
(answer below)

Mr. Tomashiro: Joseph, how was your family trip to France this summer?

Joseph: You wouldn't believe it!

Mr. Tomashiro: Why is that?

Joseph: Well, even the little kids speak French over there!

Tripping the scales at more than one hundred tons is the blue whale. It grows to more than one hundred feet long!

History!

Ms. Wong: Now, class, we will start our unit on the Middle Ages with learning about castles. But, first—Andrew, please put away your colored pencils!
Noah: But, Ms. Wong, it says *draw*bridge on the first page!

A piggy bank has nothing to do with pigs! In the Middle Ages, people stored their money in a jar made from a clay called "pygg." The jar was known as the "pygg jar." Gradually, the shape of the jar, and the name, became a pig bank, and then a "piggy bank" as it is known today.

Ms. Wong: Noah, is there a July 4 in England?
Noah: No, of course not!
Ms. Wong: Then how do they get from July 3 to July 5?

Ms. Wong: Why were the Middle Ages also called the Dark Ages?
Noah: Because there were so many knights?

Ms. Wong: What was Alexander the Great's middle name?
Noah: The.

What is the most popular museum in the world?
(answer below)

Ms. Wong: What do you call a knight who just lost a fencing match?
Noah: A sword loser.

Ms. Wong: When a castle was filled, where did knights stay overnight?
Noah: In a moat-el.

The National Air and Space Museum in Washington, D.C.
It gets ten million visitors a year!

Ms. Wong: Who was one of the most famous dancers in medieval history?
Noah: Sir Dance-a-lot!

Ms. Wong: When did the knights arrive for the sporting events?
Noah: Joust in time!

What is Washington, D.C.'s only skyscraper?
(answer below)

Ms. Wong: Where did Shakespeare like to write poems?
Noah: Under a poet-tree!

Sam: Ms. Wong, can I take my history test in the computer lab?
Ms. Wong: Why is that?
Sam: Because I can get more memory there!

Anthony: Yikes, watch out!

Ms. Wong: What's the matter, Anthony?

Anthony: A bee just flew in the window!

Ms. Wong: But, Anthony, I thought you always wanted a B in history!

Music Class!

Jane: What song has a lot of appeal?
Sylvie: "The Star Spangled Banana!"

What's the noisiest land animal?
(answer below)

Principal: Why are you walking out of music class?
Rebecca: My teacher asked if I could sing "Far, Far, Away!"

Jane: What's the difference between a piano and a fish?
Sylvie: You can tune a piano, but you can't tune a fish!

What are the notes of the C major chord?
(answer below)

Jose: Why are the cows lined up outside the door?
Jack: They're waiting to get inside moo-sic class!

From the Principal's Office!

Ms. O'Callahan: Sally, your behavior is unacceptable. Go to the principal's office!
Sally: But I'm hungry. Can I go to the cafeteria instead?

Claire: Why was Principal O'Callahan wearing red sneakers?
Christy: Because her orange ones were dirty!

What is the tallest land animal in the world?
(answer below)

Brett: Why does the king of the jungle never tell the truth?
Adam: Because he's always a lion!

No surprise here! It's the giraffe, which can grow as tall as eighteen feet.

Ms. Valenzuela: Victor, it's time for you to get up for school!

Victor: But, Mom, do I have to?
Everyone hates me and makes fun of me!
Do I have to go to school?

Ms. Valenzuela: Yes—you're the principal!

Claire: Christy, why are you doing exercises in front of the principal's office?

Christy: Because I'm going to have to stretch the truth a bit once I'm in there!

Principal: What happened to the frog who was parked illegally in front of the school?

Custodian: It got toad away!

Principal: Does the roof always leak like this?

Custodian: Only when it's raining.

From the Nurse's Office!

Nurse Perez: Kevin, how did you get to the nurse's office?
Kevin: Flu.

Imer: Why is the nurse so crabby when no one is in her office?
Flora: Because she doesn't have any patients!

Imer: Why was the nurse putting Band-Aids on her plants?
Flora: For growing pains!

Suzie: What's faster—hot or cold?
Fiona: Hot—because you can catch a cold!

Kenya: What is one thing you can never catch?
Jonah: A breeze!

Recess!

Denzil: What is the best kind of candy to eat on the playground?
Dwayne: *Recess* Pieces!

Denzil: Do you like using the slide?
Dwayne: It has its ups and downs!

Denzil: What did the elephant say when the tree fell on him during recess?
Dwayne: I guess the oaks on me!

Denzil: It must have been raining cats and dogs last night on the playground!
Dwayne: Why do you say that?
Denzil: I just stepped in a big poodle.

Gym!

Carlos: My new gym shoes are killing me.
Coach Kaplan: That's because you have them on the wrong feet!
Carlos: But these are the only feet I have!

How high is a regulation basketball hoop?
(answer below)

Coach Kaplan: Why are you always so tired for gym every day?
Toby: Because we only have gym on weakdays!

Tanya: Coach Kaplan, I can tell you the score of today's soccer game before it even starts!
Coach Kaplan: How's that!
Tanya: It's nothing to nothing!

Ten feet

Who was the first African-American to play in the Major Leagues? Extra credit if you can name his team and his number!

(answer below)

Coach Kaplan: What's the best way to catch a ball?
Tali: Have someone throw it to you.

What is a Green Bay Packer?
After playing college football for Notre Dame, Curly Lambeau went back home to Green Bay and got a job with a meat-packing company called the Indian Packing Company. Curly got this idea to start a professional football team, and he went to the president of the company and asked for a loan to buy uniforms and some equipment. In return, he promised the president of the company he would call the team the "Packers." The year was 1919, and the Packers have been "packing" them in ever since!

Jackie Robinson, Brooklyn Dodgers, number 42, in 1947.

Carl: What do you call a time-out in a Lions' football game?
Beth: A paws.

Roni: What are those little black dots standing on the first-base line before the baseball game?
Tommy: Oh, those are ants getting ready to sing the national ant-hymn!

Sherise: What's a rabbit's favorite martial arts move?
Daniel: A karate hop!

Who holds the record for most consecutive games played in baseball?

(answer below)

Cal Ripken—2,632 games over a 16-year period. He voluntarily ended his streak on Sunday, September 21, 1998.

Coach Kaplan: Tim, why are you wearing scuba gear?

Tim: I'm going to do some diving in the ocean so I can get in better shape.

Coach Kaplan: Why?

Tim: Because then I can get all the mussels that I need!

From the School Cafeteria!

Cassie: There are times when I have absolutely no appetite.
Valeria: When is that?
Cassie: Right after lunch.

Steve: What did the frog order for lunch?
Eric: A hamburger with flies.

Who was the Baby Ruth candy bar named after?
(answer below)

Cassie: If your friend gets an ice-cream sandwich and you get a bite, what should you do?
Valeria: Scratch it!

Some say that the candy bar was named after the baby daughter of President Grover Cleveland. (Grover Cleveland was the 22nd and the 24th President of the United States—1885–1889 and 1893–1897.

41

Cindy: Why did your dad buy you asparagus for lunch?
Angel: Because he couldn't get them for nothing.

Hot dogs last more than ten years in a landfill!

Ronnie: What vegetable was not welcome on the *Titanic*?
Irene: A leek.

Jai-Wai: Do you mind if I throw my trash in the barrel?
Bob: No, dump right in!

Richard: How many eggs in a dozen?
Sandra: Twelve.
Richard: Eggs-actly!

Sam: Why are the cows lined up at the door?
Max: They're waiting to get into the calf-eteria!

Gabe: What has scaly orange skin, green teeth, and drinks milk with a straw?
Harrison: Odzilla!

Principal: What should we feed the astronaut after he is finished talking at the assembly?
Francesca: Launch!

Art Class!

Ms. Watkins: Theresa, why are you crying?
Theresa: Because the directions for the art project say to "tear along the dotted line!"

Leonardo da Vinci invented scissors.

Theresa: Ms. Watkins, Clarence is being rude again!
Ms. Watkins: What seems to be the problem?
Theresa: Every time I use the scissors for my project, he makes a cutting remark!

What seven colors make up the rainbow?
(answer below)

Theresa: What did the scissors say to the paper?
Manny: I'm a cut above the rest!

Math!

What makes more noise than twenty-two screaming kids in a class?
> —twenty-three screaming kids!

How many thousands are in a million?
(answer below)

What is a caterpillar's favorite subject?
> —Mothematics!

By the Numbers!
(Quiz your teacher and friends)

1. What is the name of the famous Indiana auto race? (Indy 500)

2. How often do we have a national census? (Every ten years)

A thousand

3. What is the boiling point for water in Fahrenheit? (212 degrees above zero)

4. What is the boiling point for water in Celsius? (100 degrees above zero)

5. How many seconds in an hour? (3,600)

6. What is the freezing point of water in centigrade? (Zero)

7. How many days in a fortnight?
(Fourteen days)

8. How long did Rip Van Winkle sleep?
(Twenty years)

9. President Lincoln's famous speech, the Gettysburg Address, begins "Four score and seven years ago . . ." How much is this?
("Score" stands for twenty years.
4 x 20 = 80 years; 80 + 7 = 87)

10. How many steps in the Washington Monument? (898)

11. How long is a football field? (100 yards/300 feet)

12. How many squares on a checkerboard? (Sixty-four)

13. How many United States senators are there? (One hundred)

14. How many members of the House of Representatives are there? (435)

15. How many United States Supreme Court justices are there? (Nine)

16. How often do we have a leap year? (Every four years)

Aaron: Why was six afraid of seven?
Tara: Because seven eight nine!

Ms. Bonelli: What is never part of anything?
Stefan: The "whole."

Rudy: Why does Ms. Bonelli looks so sad?
Ashley: Because she has so many problems to solve!

Ms. Bonelli: What's the difference between an old quarter and a new nickel?
Stefan: Twenty cents.

Andy: Which month has twenty-eight days?
Brent: All of them.

Ms. Bonelli: Why are you crying, Stefan? The math test isn't *that* hard!

Stefan: You're standing on my toe!

Science!

Raymond: What do you call two happy falcons?
Spike: A pair-of-grins.

*What kind of lizard can change its color
to match its surroundings?*
(answer "A" below)

One drippy faucet wastes ten thousand gallons of water in a year! Are there any drippy faucets in your school or home?

Cindy: Are there earthquakes on Mars?
Becky: No, but there are Marsquakes!

What is a squab?
(answer "B" below)

A: Chameleon. B: A baby pigeon.

Ricky: What did one whale say to the other whale when he was in trouble?
Gabe: I need kelp!

Ms. Haddad: That butterfly used to be a caterpillar.
Ricky: I thought it looked familiar!

What's the fastest animal of all (it's even faster than the cheetah)? Hint—it has wings.

(answer below)

Victor: Why do you like studying about volcanoes?
Tony: It's a lava fun!

Ms. Haddad: Chris, do you like learning about frogs in science?
Chris: Toad-ally!

The spinetail swift. It can reach straight ahead speed at 105 miles per hour! But, when the peregrin falcon dives, it can reach speeds up to 204 miles per hour.

If you're looking for the biggest volcano in the solar system, things are looking up! It's called Olympus Mons and it's on Mars. It's also almost three times the size of Mount Everest.

Gabriel: Did you know that water freezes at 32 degrees Fahrenheit (0 degrees Celsius) when it gets too cold to stay liquid?
Carl: That's nothing. I reached my boiling point just this morning when my homework fell out of my backpack right into the mud.

What is a baby kangaroo called?
(answer below)

Ms. Haddad: Patrick, why are you wearing a diving mask and flippers in school?
Patrick: Because you told us that two-thirds of a person's body weight is water!

Billy: What kind of money do marsupials use?
Imer: Pocket change.

A joey

Saroush: How does the Man-in-the-Moon hold up his pants?
Cal: With an asteroid belt!

Lebanon, Kansas, is the geographical center of the United States. Ruby, North Dakota, is the geographical center of North America.

What's an emu?

(answer below)

Gabriel: Did you know that an echo happens when sound waves are blocked by a hard surface like the side of a mountain?
Carlos: I know, I know, I know, I know, I know, I know . . .

Andy: What do you call a bear who got caught in the rain?
Rebecca: A drizzly bear!

A large Australian non-flying bird that looks like an ostrich, but smaller.

Sam: Why do whales like to swim in the ocean?
Daniella: For the krill of it!

Can you name the earth's five oceans—in order, from largest to smallest?
(answer below)

Gabriel: What's wrong with that fish in Ms. Haddad's aquarium?
Carl: It has a haddock!

Rainbows form when sunlight passes through drops of water.

Rebecca: What do you call a boring fish?
Roberto: A dull-fin!

Chris: I just read that forests cover 34 percent of the earth!
Aaron: Wood you believe it?

Pacific (it's almost twice the size of the Atlantic! It covers 32 percent of the whole earth!), Atlantic, Indian, Antarctic, and Arctic.

Robby: What's at the center of Earth?
William: *r*

55

From what two metals is bronze made?
(answer below)

Chris: How can you carry water in a net?
Aaron: Freeze it!

The Dead Sea, on the Israel-Jordan border, is the saltiest sea in the world!

Field Trip!

At the Aquarium!

Kristen: What did one fish say to the other fish?
Karen: Long time, no sea!

Charlotte: What did one fish say to the other fish who was swimming by itself?
Julia: Why aren't you in school?

What does scuba stand for?
(answer below)

Imer: Why are oceans friendly?
Fred: Because they always wave.

At the Playground!

Abbey: Did you have fun on the swings?
Jordan: It had its ups and downs.

Self-Contained Underwater Breathing Apparatus

Abbey: How did you find the weather on the playground?
Jordan: Easy, I went outside and there it was.

Chloe: Why are you walking so softly on the playground?
Ben: I don't want to break any of the plates of rock that make up the earth's surface!

At the Park!

Michael: How can a class of twenty-three kids, one teacher, one aide, and four parent chaperones stand under one umbrella and not get wet?
Jordan: It's not raining!

A Harbor Cruise!

Ms. Berman: Tomorrow we are taking a boat ride around the harbor. What are you going to say to the captain when we step aboard his boat?
Theresa: Hull-o!

School Daze!

Angel: What smells most in a school?
Seth: Your nose.

Tali: Why are you standing in front of the wall clock with a fly swatter?
Max: I'm watching time flies!

Koby: Why are you taking the money from our bake sale on that sled?
Lauren: Because I'm going to the snowbank!

*Can you name all the dwarfs in the
Disney movie Snow White?*

(answer below)

Sasha: Why are you taking the money from the school raffle in that canoe?
Angela: Because I'm going to the riverbank!

Bashful, Doc, Dopey, Grumpy, Happy, Sleepy, and Sneezy

Karen: Which month has twenty-eight days?
Tommy: All of them!

What word rhymes with month?

(answer below)

Karen: What comes once in a minute, once in a month, but never in a day?
Tommy: The letter *m*!

After School!

Ms. Martinez: Are you meeting your daughter, Stephanie, after school?
Mom: Oh no, I've known her for years!

Shana: Why is the turtle always the first one home after school?
Cassie: Because it carries its house on its back!

Sam: When did you lose your notebook?
Rebecca: When I couldn't find it anymore.

Sam: Where did you lose your notebook?
Rebecca: It depends on where I lost it.

Sam: What is the best time to make a dentist appointment?
Rebecca: Tooth-hurty!

At Home Again!

Dad: How come you didn't change your clothes for baseball practice?
Letitia: I changed my mind instead!

Kayla: What's the best thing to eat when you're behind in your homework?
Sean: Ketchup!

Mom: A rabbit's house is called a warren, alligators have nests, and foxes live in dens. What do you call your room?
Letitia: A mess.

Devon: What do parents and teachers have in common?
Jevon: They both give homework!

Why is a bad joke like a broken pencil?
— **It has no point.**